HILLTOP ELEMENTARY SCHOOL

W9-CBT-657

# BENJAMIN McFADDEN AND THE ROBOT BABYSITTER

TIMOTHY BUSH

CROWN BOOKS  NEW YORK

For Ruthann Enthoff, my own Ultimate Babysitter.

With thanks to Anne Marie and Calvin for significant aid and comfort along the way.

I'll buy you each an asteroid if I ever get the money.

Copyright © 1998 by Timothy Bush

All rights reserved. No part of this book may be reproduced or transmitted in any form or by any means,
electronic or mechanical, including photocopying, recording, or by any information storage and retrieval system,
without permission in writing from the publisher.

Published by Crown Publishers, Inc., a Random House company, 201 East 50th Street, New York, NY 10022

CROWN is a trademark of Crown Publishers, Inc.
www.randomhouse.com/kids/
Printed in Singapore

*Library of Congress Cataloging-in-Publication Data*
Bush, Timothy.
Benjamin McFadden and the robot babysitter / Timothy Bush. —1st ed.
p.     cm.
Summary: When Benjamin McFadden reprograms his robot Babysitter to be more fun, he discovers that there is such a thing as too much fun.
[1. Robots—Fiction. 2. Babysitters—Fiction. 3. Science fiction.] I. Title.
PZ7.B96545Be        1998
[E]—dc21        97-52589
ISBN 0-517-79984-7 (trade)
0-517-79985-5 (lib. bdg.)

10 9 8 7 6 5 4 3

# THE NIGHT HIS MOTHER AND FATHER WENT OUT

to the Rings of Saturn Preservation Dance, Benjamin McFadden and his kitten, Fantastic, were not invited to come along.

"Grownups only," his father said. "And haven't you got homework in Creative Computing?"

"I hate that class," said Benjamin McFadden. "I think my teacher is an alien spy."

But his parents flew off in their silver ship, and Benjamin McFadden was left alone with his terrible robot Babysitter.

"8:00 Earth time," Babysitter said. "My programming tells me that it's time for you to sleep."

"Programming's wrong," answered Benjamin McFadden. "I'm always allowed to stay up till ten."

"Bed," said Babysitter.

"No," said Benjamin.

But Babysitter wouldn't take no for an answer.

Benjamin put his pajamas on. He put his pajamas on very slowly.

"8:15 Earth time," Babysitter said. "You are now in violation of your scheduled routine."

"May I have a cookie?" Benjamin asked.

"No," said Babysitter. "Time for bed."

Benjamin folded his arms and said, "The trouble with you, Babysitter, is that you are no fun."

Babysitter answered, "I'm not programmed for fun."

Benjamin McFadden said, "We'll see about that."

Benjamin opened up the panel on Babysitter's back, which his parents
had told him he should never, *never* do. He tried what he'd learned in
Creative Computing and reprogrammed Babysitter to be more fun.

"What time is it, Babysitter?" Benjamin asked.

"8:20 Earth time," Babysitter said. "My programming tells me that it's time for fun. Benjamin McFadden, what is fun?"

Benjamin McFadden was happy to explain.

"Games," said Benjamin. "Games are fun.
But two arms per player, or it isn't fair."

"Books," said Benjamin. "Books are fun. They never need batteries, they fit in your knapsack, and when they get broken, you can fix them with tape."

"Music," said Benjamin. "Music is fun.
Anyone can make it, and the louder the better."

All that explaining made him hungry. Benjamin decided it was time to eat.
"Cookies," he said, and Babysitter brought them.
"Cake," he said, and out it came.
"Waffles."
"Burgers."
"Milk shakes."
"Fries."
Babysitter gave him everything he wanted. Babysitter told him, "This is fun!"

Lots of fun plus lots of food equaled a suddenly sleepy boy.

"That's enough, Babysitter," Benjamin said. "I think I'm ready to go to bed."

"9:05 Earth time," Babysitter said. "Programming tells me it's time for fun."

"No," said Benjamin. "I *want* to go to bed." But Babysitter wouldn't take no for an answer.

"The trouble with you, Benjamin McFadden, is that you are no fun. Humans get tired, but robots do not. I will build fun robots. Fun must be had."

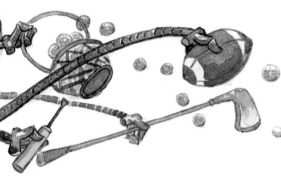

"Games!" said Babysitter. "Games are fun."

"Books!" said Babysitter. "Books are fun."

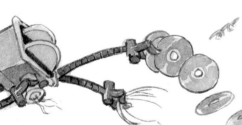

"Music is fun . . .

. . . and food is fun!"

And all the robots answered . . .

"Fun!"

But Benjamin McFadden didn't think it was fun. He only wanted to go to bed. He tried to put Babysitter's programming back, but somehow that only made things worse.

"Fun time! Fun time!" Babysitter said. "Fun time! Fun time! Fun, fun, *fun!*"

Benjamin McFadden called for help.

"Babysitter Help Line," a lady answered. Benjamin tried to explain what was wrong.

"I don't understand it." The lady frowned. "Our company's robots are very reliable."

Benjamin confessed that he'd opened up the back.

"That is very serious," the lady told him. "You should never, *never* open up your Babysitter's back."

"I know that now," groaned Benjamin McFadden.

"But how can I get my Babysitter under control?"

The lady from the Babysitter Help Line explained, "Babysitter robots have an Ultimate Password, which restarts their original program. Once the original program restarts, your robot ought to function normally again."

"But I don't know any Ultimate Password!"

"Just a minute," the lady said. "We should have it on file . . . Yes! Here it is."

But before the lady could tell him the password, Babysitter took the phone away.

"Fun!" said Babysitter. "Fun! Fun! Fun!" And Benjamin McFadden was on his own.

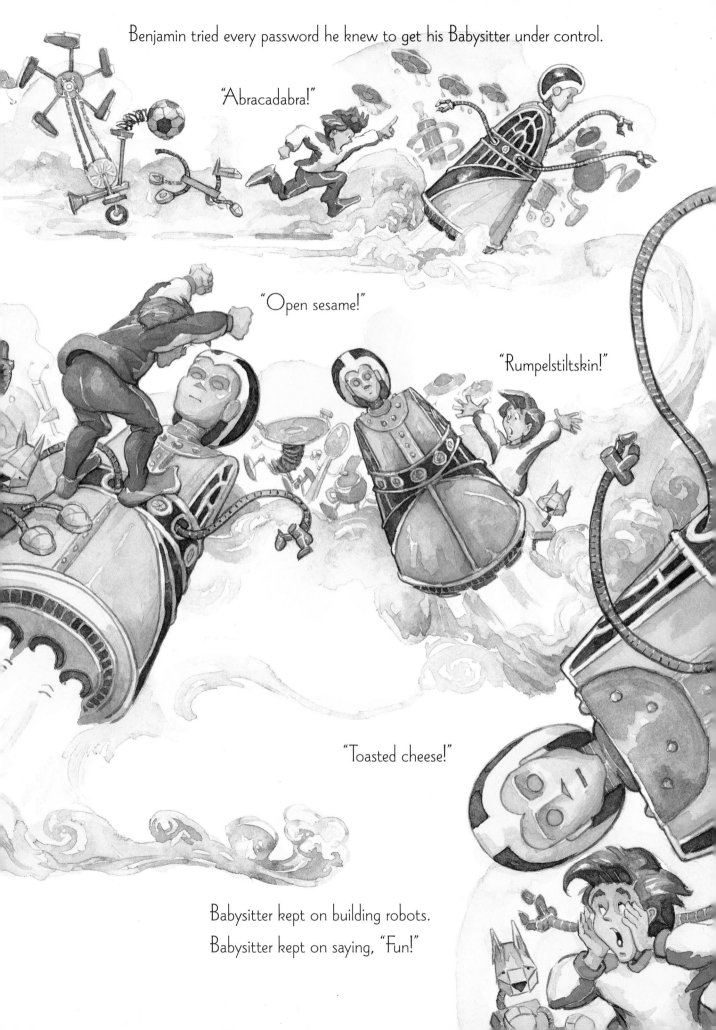

Benjamin tried every password he knew to get his Babysitter under control.

"Abracadabra!"

"Open sesame!"

"Rumpelstiltskin!"

"Toasted cheese!"

Babysitter kept on building robots.
Babysitter kept on saying, "Fun!"

Benjamin tried the names of the planets.
The names of all the planets' moons. He
named the stars and the constellations and
the capital cities of Earth and Mars.

He was starting on comets and
asteroids when Babysitter suddenly
snatched Fantastic.

"Put down my kitten!" yelled Benjamin McFadden, and grabbed
hold of Fantastic's tail. "You put him down, Babysitter, or you know
what I'll do? I'll tell! . . . I'll tell my *parents* on you!"

"Parents?" said Babysitter. Everything stopped.

"Parents?" said the other robots, looking around.

"Parents!" said Benjamin McFadden.

"Parents!"

And that, of course, was the Ultimate Password.

Babysitter's original program restarted.

"12:20 Earth time," Babysitter said. "You ought to be in bed now, Benjamin McFadden."

Fantastic and Benjamin went to bed. It wasn't easy to fall asleep because Babysitter was taking all the robots apart. Babysitter put all the pieces back and cleaned up after all the fun.

Benjamin McFadden was still awake when his mother and father came home in their ship.

"How did it go?" he heard them ask.

Babysitter's programming must have been slow, because Babysitter's answer was a long time coming.

"My memory tells me there is nothing to report. Benjamin McFadden is an excellent child."

His parents looked into Benjamin's room, but Benjamin pretended to be asleep. They tiptoed over to kiss his forehead, then they tiptoed out again.

Benjamin McFadden sat up in bed. "What a weird night," he said to Fantastic.

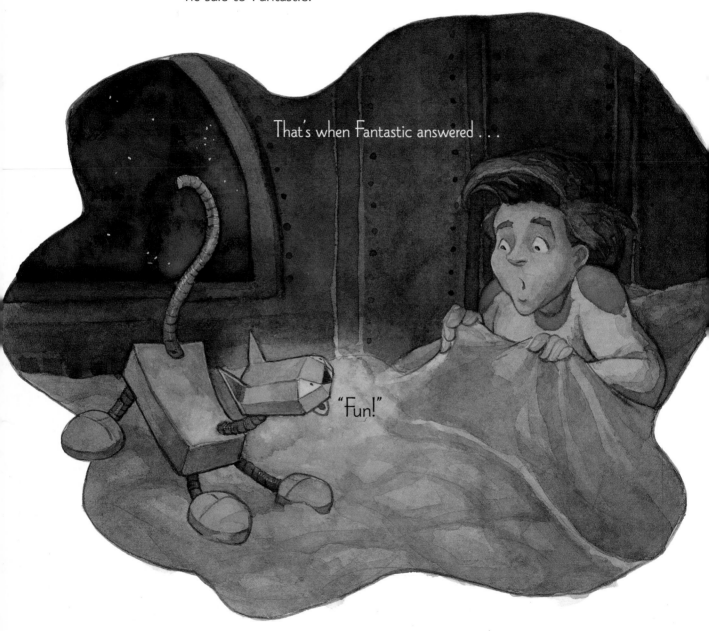

That's when Fantastic answered . . .

"Fun!"

HILLTOP ELEMENTARY SCHOOL,

HILLTOP ELEMENTARY SCHOOL,